PLAZA

DATE DUE

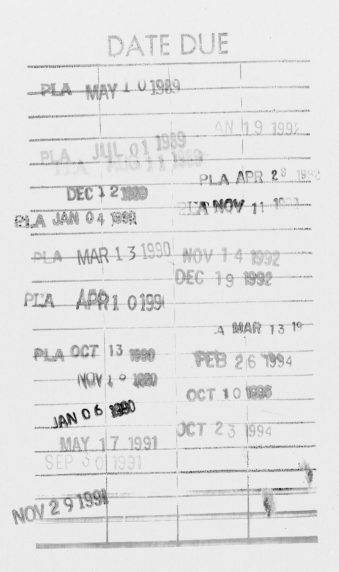

THE MAGIC LEAF

To Philip Klindt—without him,
this book would not have
happened

The Magic Leaf

by Winifred Morris

illustrated by Ju-Hong Chen

Atheneum   1987   New York

Atheneum
Macmillan Publishing Company
866 Third Avenue, New York, NY 10022

Type set by V&M Graphics, New York City.
Printed and bound by Toppan Printing Company, Japan
Typography by Mary Ahern. Calligraphy by Jeanyee Wong
First Edition.

10   9   8   7   6   5   4   3   2   1

Library of Congress Cataloging-in-Publication Data

Morris, Winifred.   The magic leaf.

SUMMARY: When a foolish man believes he has become
invisible by possessing a magic leaf, he sneaks into the
mayor's private garden to view the peonies.
* [1. Folklore—China] I. Chen, Ju-Hong, ill.*
II. Title.
PZ8.1.M8342Mag   1987   398.2'1'0951   86-28898
ISBN 0-689-31358-6

In northeast China, a long time ago, there was a man named Lee Foo who was both
a swordsman and a scholar.

He was a smart looking man. When he traveled
across the lake on his way to the town, he stood
very tall in his boat. And his sword swung bravely
at his hip.

But one day, his sword fell into the water.
He watched it sink away from him. He watched
it nestle into the rocks at the bottom of the lake.

He was very upset, of course,
but he was sure that a smart
fellow like himself should
be able to think of what to do.
And, indeed, he came up
with a plan.

He leaned over and made
a mark on the side
of the boat. He made the mark
exactly where the
sword had fallen
into the water.

Then he went on his way. Now he knew where his sword was, and he could get it any time.

But the next day, when he returned to the lake and dove into the water right where the mark was on the side of the boat, for some reason, he couldn't find his sword.

Some time later, Lee Foo noticed that he needed
a new pair of shoes. Again, he put a lot of thought
into the matter.

First, he found a piece of paper—because he firmly believed
that any project should be started with a piece of paper. He
put his foot on the paper, and carefully he drew around it.

"Someone not as smart as myself might leave it to chance to find a pair of shoes that would fit him," he said. "But with this drawing of my foot, I will be able to find a pair of shoes that will fit me exactly."

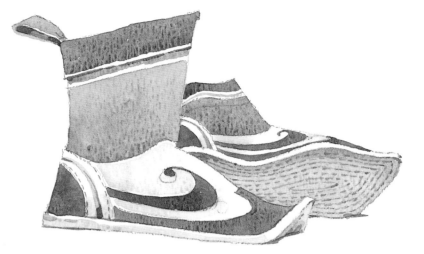

Then he went to the market, where he looked
through all the stalls of all the shoemakers until
he found a handsome pair of shoes
that he liked very much.

But when he reached into his shirt, he discovered he had forgotten his piece of paper! He had forgotten his outline! So, of course, he couldn't buy the shoes. How would he know if they fit?

Instead he had to hurry home. He had to find the outline.

But by the time he got back to the market place, the shoemaker was gone. He stood alone in the empty street and watched the few remaining shopkeepers pack up their stalls for the night.

Then he had to return home in his ragged old shoes.

For all his mishaps, Lee Foo never doubted the fact that he was a very smart man. Did he not read very big books the way smart men are supposed to do?

One day he found a book that was so big and so heavy that he could hardly lift it into his lap. He could hardly hold it to turn the pages. It was an ancient book of magic—for in those days in China the study of magic was taken very seriously. Lee Foo was sure that such a big, heavy book must hold wonderful secrets.

And it was true. The book did tell of amazing things. The book said that with a certain magic leaf, a person could make himself invisible. The book told how to find the magic leaf, and it did not sound difficult to Lee Foo. According to the book, it was the leaf the praying mantis hides under when it waits to catch the cicada.

Now it was summer, and praying mantises and cicadae were everywhere in the fields. Lee Foo was sure he would be able to find the magic leaf.

And, of course, he was right. Only a little way from his house, he lifted a leaf, and there was a praying mantis hiding under it.

Quickly he picked it. But, in his excitement, he dropped it. The magic leaf now lay on the ground in a pile of many, many leaves, and they all looked alike.

"Oh, no!" said Lee Foo. "But a smart person like myself should be able to figure out which leaf is the magic one."

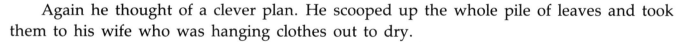

Again he thought of a clever plan. He scooped up the whole pile of leaves and took them to his wife who was hanging clothes out to dry.

"Look what I have found!" he said proudly. "Soon I will be able to do anything I want!" Then he picked up one of the leaves, he held it in front of him, and he asked her, "Can you see me now?"

His wife was puzzled by her husband's enthusiasm over a pile of leaves, but she said, "Yes. Yes, of course, I can see you."

"Oh, well. Then it isn't that one," said Lee Foo, and he tossed it over his shoulder.

Quickly he picked up another leaf. "Now can you see me?" he said.

And again his wife said, "Yes. Yes, of course, I can see you." So he threw the second leaf aside.

The pile of leaves was very large. His wife finished hanging up the clothes. She went into the kitchen to roll out the dough for the noodles. And Lee Foo scurried along behind her, still carrying his wonderful pile of leaves, and still pulling leaves one by one from the pile.

"Yes," his wife kept saying. And "Yes," again. "Yes, I can still see you." And another "Yes."

Until she tired of turning around. Then, without looking at him, in a weary voice, she said, "No. No, I can't see you now."

"*Ah ha!*" cried Lee Foo.

Now that he knew that he could make himself invisible, Lee Foo began to think about what he could do with this great power.

And he thought of the mayor's garden.

The mayor was much too rich to live in the small town, but he had built a garden there, just to show how rich he was. It was said to be a magnificent garden of peonies, for in China the peony grows as a tree and is a symbol of wealth and nobility. But Lee Foo had never seen it. None of the common people of the town had seen the garden, for it was hidden behind a high wall.

When he was a boy, Lee Foo had tried to peek through the gate. He had tried to climb the trees near the high wall. But the mayor's guards had always chased him away. He hadn't much liked those guards. And the more he thought about the garden that was hidden behind the forbidding wall, and the more he thought about the way the guards had chased him, the more pleased he was with the idea of using his magic leaf to walk right past those unfriendly guards.

When he got to the garden, the gate was open. The guards were laughing together some distance away. Lee Foo smiled, held his leaf tightly, and entered the garden.

Immediately the guards turned and shouted, but Lee Foo didn't worry. Immediately the guards began running right toward him, but still Lee Foo didn't worry.

He strolled along the gravel paths. He stopped at each peony to admire its color, for each one was different. He was enjoying a lovely deep purple one when the guards seized him and dragged him off to jail.

There he spent a
long, lonely night
wondering what could
have gone wrong.

The next day, when he was brought before the judge, he explained that there had been a mistake. "The guards should not have seized me in the garden, your honor, for I was invisible at the time!"

He told the judge about the big, heavy book. He told the judge about the magic leaf and the praying mantis. "And then I tried every leaf," he said, "until my wife told me she couldn't see me."

The judge listened closely. Then he asked to see the book.

He too believed in magic and big, heavy books, so he studied the book very carefully. Then he asked to see the leaf.

And the judge studied the leaf very carefully also. He turned it from side to side, holding it in front of him with two bony fingers.

"Can you see me now?" he said.

Lee Foo looked down at his side where he used to wear his sword so proudly. He wiggled his toes, which were poking out of his old, tattered shoes. He thought about his long, lonely night in jail, and he didn't feel very smart just then.

He had enjoyed the mayor's garden, but not that much.

He was looking at the guards, who were eager to take him back to jail when he said, "No. No, your honor. I can't see you now."

Then the judge said, "*Ah ha!*"

So the judge let Lee Foo go home, but he kept the magic leaf. He said he needed it as evidence.

Lee Foo was so glad to go home that he didn't mind losing the leaf. He was no longer interested in clever plans, and he no longer thought of himself as a very smart man.

So maybe he was smarter than he had been before.